DreamWorks

TrollHunters

Tales of Arcadia

from Guillermo del Toro

DREAMWORKS

TROLLHUNTERS

TALES OF ARCADIA

FROM GUILLERMO DEL TORO

THE FELLED

Script by
RICHARD ASHLEY HAMILTON

Pages 5–7, 17–27, 37–52, 62–70

Pencils by
TIMOTHY GREEN II

Inks by
JOE SILVER

Coloring by
WES DZIOBA

Pages 8–16, 28–36, 53–61

Art by
OMAR LOZANO

Coloring by
EDGAR DELGADO

Lettering by
RICHARD STARKINGS and
Comicraft's JIMMY BETANCOURT

Cover Art by
TIMOTHY GREEN II and
JOE SILVER with WES DZIOBA

Dark Horse Books

HUMAN TEENAGER JIM LAKE, JR., POSSESSES THE MAGICAL AMULET THAT GIVES HIM A POWERFUL SUIT OF ARMOR AND THE MONUMENTAL RESPONSIBILITY OF TROLLHUNTER—DEFENDER OF THE GOOD TROLLS. ALONG WITH HIS FRIENDS—BOTH HUMAN AND TROLL—HE TRAINS TO FIGHT FOR THE TROLLS THAT LIVE BENEATH HIS HOMETOWN OF ARCADIA OAKS.

**The events in this story take place immediately after* Trollhunters *Episode 207, "Hero with a Thousand Faces"*

HEARTSTONE TROLLMARKET.
I THOUGHT THE ASPECTUS STONE WAS SUPPOSED TO MULTIPLY MY STRENGTH--
--NOT MULTIPLY MY PROBLEMS!

BAD TIME AT CLAIRE'S *FAJITA?*
UM, I THINK YOU MEAN ***FIESTA,*** AAARRRGGHH!!!
BUT, YEAH, LET'S JUST SAY I'M PROBABLY FACING A LIFETIME ***BAN*** FROM *CASA DE NUÑEZ.*

OH, COME NOW, MASTER JIM. SURELY THIS PRIMITIVE HUMAN ***"BAR-BUH-CUE"*** RITUAL YOU ATTENDED MUST HAVE OFFERED ***SOME*** REDEEMING ELEMENT?
WELL...CLAIRE DID REFER TO ME AS HER ***BOYFRIEND.***
AH, YOU SEE! THIS IS MERELY ANOTHER EXAMPLE OF YOU ***SECOND-GUESSING*** YOURSELF!

YOU HAVE ***NO*** IDEA.
...THE ASPECTUS STONE MADE ME ***CONFRONT*** ALL THESE DIFFERENT SIDES OF MY PERSONALITY. SURE, I REINED 'EM ALL IN...EVENTUALLY, BUT...
HOW GOOD OF A BOYFRIEND CAN I BE IF I CAN'T EVEN FIGURE OUT WHO I ***REALLY*** AM?

I MEAN, DON'T I NEED TO KNOW MYSELF BEFORE I CAN BE THERE FOR CLAIRE? OR ANYONE ELSE.
ALL FASCINATING QUESTIONS, TROLLHUNTER. LET'S ANSWER THEM TOMORROW.
TONIGHT'S ALL-YOU-CAN-GLUG NIGHT AT THE PUB...
REALLY, VENDEL?

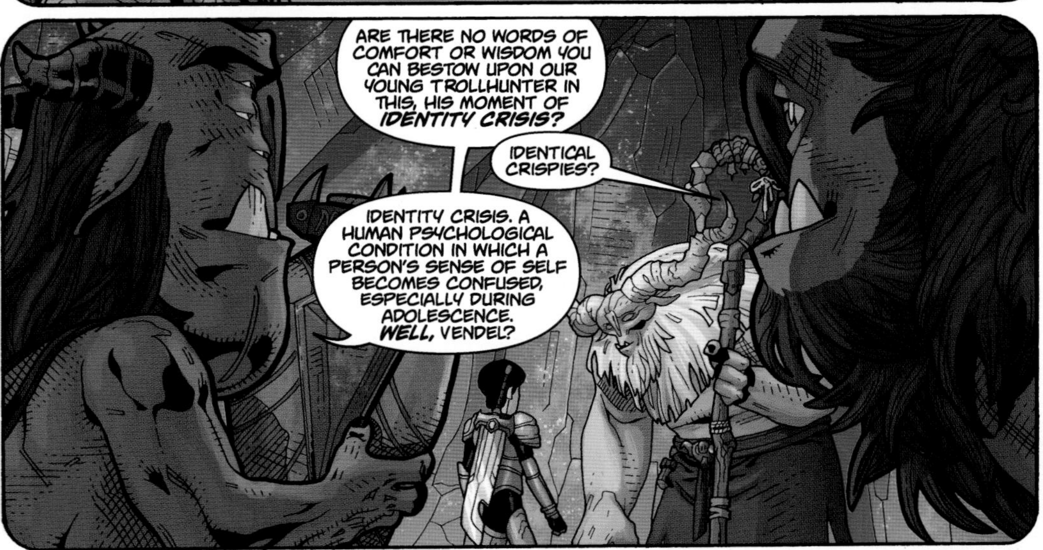
ARE THERE NO WORDS OF COMFORT OR WISDOM YOU CAN BESTOW UPON OUR YOUNG TROLLHUNTER IN THIS, HIS MOMENT OF IDENTITY CRISIS?
IDENTICAL CRISPIES?
IDENTITY CRISIS. A HUMAN PSYCHOLOGICAL CONDITION IN WHICH A PERSON'S SENSE OF SELF BECOMES CONFUSED, ESPECIALLY DURING ADOLESCENCE. WELL, VENDEL?

FINE, FINE. LET'S ALL PUT ASIDE OUR INDIVIDUAL PLANS AND TALK ABOUT THE FLESHLING'S FEELINGS FOR HOURS ON END.
THAT'LL BE FAR MORE SATISFYING THAN A TALL, FROSTY, BOTTOMLESS FLAGON OF GLUG...

BEHOLD, THE ANAMNESIS STONE.
RENOWNED FOR ITS POWER TO RECORD MEMORIES, THIS GEM ALLOWS THE SKILLED TROLL TO CONTEMPLATE THE PRESENT BY WITNESSING THE PAST.
FOR YOU SEE, TROLLHUNTER, YOU ARE NOT THE FIRST OF MERLIN'S CHAMPIONS TO QUESTION HIS-- OR HER--TRUE NATURE...

"BEFORE KANJIGAR, EVEN BEFORE THE DAYS OF GOGUN, TROLLKIND WAS PROTECTED BY ONE OF ITS MOST CELEBRATED HEROES..."
MADDRUX THE MANY!
WHAT'S MY NAME?
MADDRUX THE MANY!
I CAN'T HEAR YOU!
MADDRUX THE MANY!
"SO NAMED FOR DISCOVERING THE VERY SAME ASPECTUS STONE YOU RELINQUISHED, SHE CULTIVATED A REPUTATION AS A CAPABLE--AND CONFIDENT--CHAMPION."

ATNUR! ABDWEN! WHEN'S THAT BABY OF YOURS GONNA GET HERE?
AS SOON AS GORGUS WILLS IT, WE SUPPOSE!
NOTHING ESCAPES YOUR GAZE--
--DOES IT, MADDRUX?
TROLLHUNTER...
ALL RIGHT, WHAT GOES ON HERE? ANOTHER SURPRISE PARTY IN MY HONOR? YOU SHOULDN'T HAVE!
THEN AGAIN, I SUPPOSE I SHOULDN'T HAVE FLATTENED THAT ENTIRE PLATOON OF GUMM-GUMMS. CAN I HELP IT IF I'M--

--SURROUNDED?
I SUPPOSE IT IS A SURPRISE PARTY OF SORTS, TROLLHUNTER--
--IF YOU CONSIDER YOUR OWN FUNERAL TO BE AN OCCASION FOR REVELRY.
I CERTAINLY INTEND TO DANCE UPON YOUR PETRIFIED REMAINS. I WILL GRIND WHAT'S LEFT OF YOUR BONES TO DUST!

ORLAGK THE OPPRESSOR. YOU MAY NOT HAVE THE SAME KNACK FOR DEATH THREATS AS YOUR GENERAL--
--BUT I'LL GIVE YOU CREDIT FOR SUCCESSFULLY INFILTRATING GLASTONBERRY TOR TROLLMARKET.
TRUE, GUNMAR POSSESSES A CERTAIN WIT, BUT EVEN HE HAS NEVER OBTAINED ONE OF YOUR HORNGAZELS.
IT MADE ENTERING THIS TROLLMARKET QUITE SIMPLE--JUST AS THE TROLL WHO ONCE HELD IT MADE QUITE THE TASTY MORSEL.

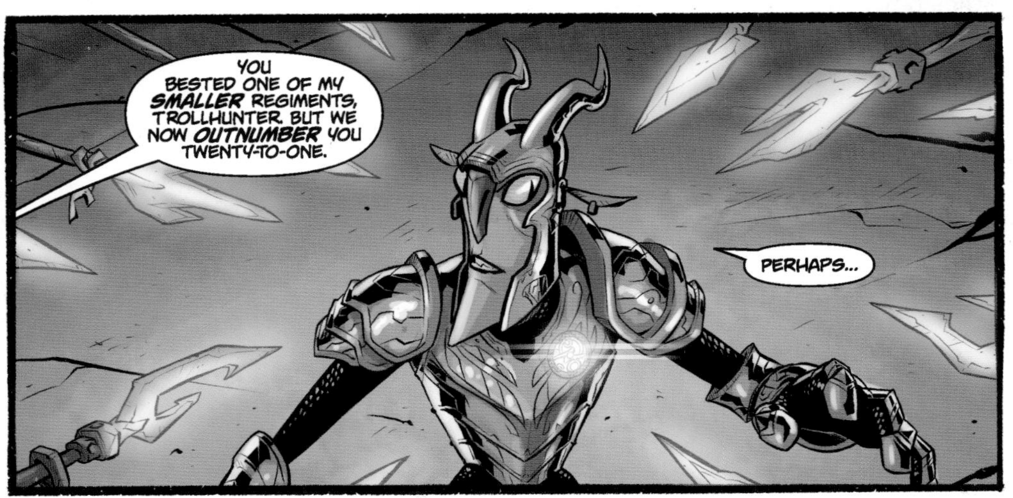
YOU BESTED ONE OF MY SMALLER REGIMENTS, TROLLHUNTER. BUT WE NOW OUTNUMBER YOU TWENTY-TO-ONE.
PERHAPS...

OR PERHAPS NOT.
OR PERHAPS NOT.
OR PERHAPS NOT.
OR PERHAPS NOT.
OR PERHAPS NOT.
OR PERHAPS NOT.

YOUR FIRST MISTAKE WAS SNEAKING INTO MY *HOME,* ORLAGK.
AND YOUR SECOND WAS *UNDERESTIMATING* ME AND MY--
UM...

ACTUALLY, HAVE YOU EVER CONSIDERED THAT MAYBE *WE'RE* UNDERESTIMATING *THEM?*
I MEAN, THERE'S SO *MANY* GUMM-GUMMS. NOT JUST HERE, BUT ON THE *SURFACE WORLD,* TOO.
DO WE--DO *I*--HAVE WHAT IT TAKES TO STOP *ALL* OF THEM?

UH, DO YOU REALLY THINK NOW IS THE BEST TIME TO HAVE THIS CONVERSATION?
JUST KEEP YOUR INSECURITIES WHERE THEY BELONG-- BURIED DEEP DOWN-- ESPECIALLY IN FRONT OF THE ENEMY!
BUT SHE DOES HAVE A POINT--
--WHAT IF THEY FIND OUT THE TRUTH ABOUT US?
YEAH! ARE WE REALLY THAT ASSURED? OR IS THIS ALL JUST AN ACT TO COVER UP THE SCARED LITTLE TROLL UNDER THE ARMOR?
HA!
NO! DON'T THINK LIKE THAT! AND IF YOU DON'T BELIEVE ME--IF YOU DON'T BELIEVE IN YOURSELVES--
--THEN TRUST IN THE AMULET. IT CHOSE US FOR A REASON. WE--I-- MAY FEEL SCARED SOMETIMES. SMALL.

BUT IF WE PUSH PAST THAT, WE CAN...
SHUNK
SHUNK
RRRMMMBBBBBBLLLLL
...MOVE MOUNTAINS.
A MOST HELPFUL SUGGESTION, TROLLHUNTER. BURYING YOUR MANY INSECURITIES DEEP DOWN...
FWOOOOMP

MAKE READY TO PILLAGE WITHOUT ME, MY BROTHERS.
FOR YOUR KING SHALL REMAIN HERE TO CATCH MERLIN'S AMULET BEFORE IT FLIES TO ITS NEXT BEARER.
WHA--?!
CRIK
IK
AK
GUMM-GUMMS! TO ME! PRIME YOUR PARLOK SPEARS! SHE MAY HAVE SUMMONED EVEN MORE DUPLICATES!

NAH... IT'S JUST ME.
CHOOOOOM
LAUGH ALL YOU WANT. SO MY SECRET'S OUT. SO YOU KNOW I QUESTION MYSELF. SO WHAT?
I DON'T HAVE TO PROVE ANYTHING TO YOU. OR MYSELVES. NOT NOW. NOT EVER AGAIN.
KLA-TANG
"ORLAGK DID MANAGE TO ESCAPE THAT DAY, ONLY TO MEET HIS OWN GRISLY DEMISE AT GUNMAR'S TREACHEROUS CLAWS SOME TIME LATER.
"BUT IN THOSE INTERVENING CENTURIES, THE GUMM-GUMMS UNDERSTOOD THAT MADDRUX'S MIGHT STEMMED NOT FROM HER MULTIPLES, BUT FROM THE ACCEPTANCE OF HER--"
"WHHHAAAAAAAAAAAAAAAAA AAAAAAAAAAAAAAAA--"

--AAAAAAAAAAAAAAAAA!
YOU SURE YOU DON'T WANNA HANG ONTO THAT ASPECTUS STONE THERE, JIMBO?

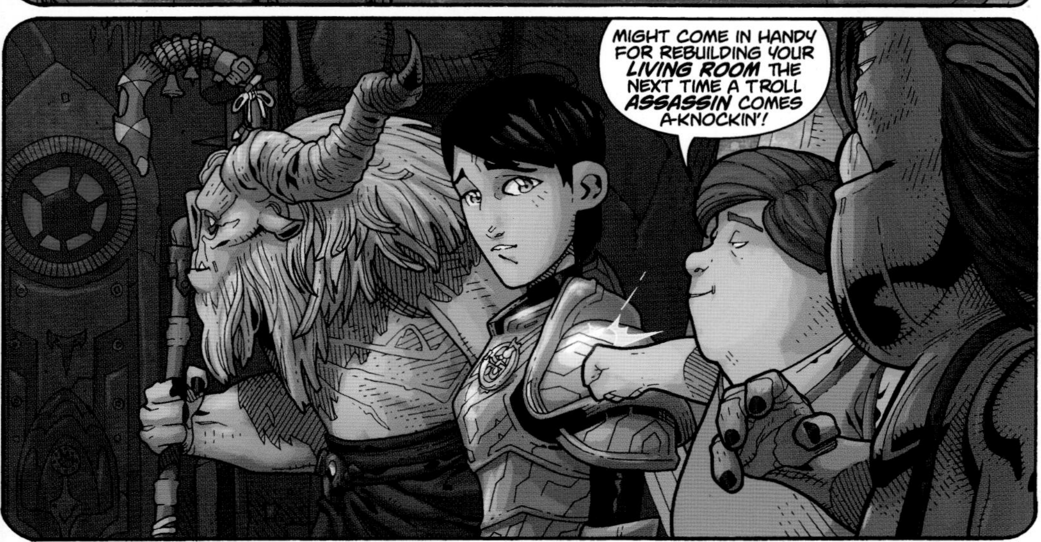
MIGHT COME IN HANDY FOR REBUILDING YOUR LIVING ROOM THE NEXT TIME A TROLL ASSASSIN COMES A-KNOCKIN'!

I'D NORMALLY TAKE GREAT UMBRAGE AT THE ROTUND FLESHLING'S INTERRUPTION. BUT PERHAPS IT'S A SIGN FROM GORGUS THAT I CAN STILL MAKE LAST CALL...
VENDEL, I GET WHAT YOU WERE SAYING ABOUT MADDRUX THE MANY. BUT THERE WAS SOMETHING ONE OF MY MULTIPLES TOLD ME EARLIER:
"THERE WILL COME A TIME YOU'LL REALIZE YOU CAN'T BALANCE BOTH WORLDS, AND YOU'LL HAVE TO CHOOSE."
SIGH SO BE IT.
AWESOMESAUCE!

"I WILL VERY BRIEFLY RECOUNT HOW ANOTHER FELLED TROLLHUNTER OF YORE STRUGGLED TO BALANCE THE TWO WORLDS HE WAS SWORN TO PROTECT... AND OTHER WORLDS ENTIRELY."

OOOOOKAY...

KLEB!
EH?

<YOU THERE! WHAT MANNER OF **TROLL** BE YOU?>
<WHOA! AND I THOUGHT THE **LOCALS** WERE FUNNY-LOOKING ON **SIRIUS-8**!>
<HOLD ON, STOP SPOUTING GIBBERISH. MY AMULET NEEDS A MOMENT TO **TRANSLATE** YOU.>
<UGH, YOUR VOICE SOUNDS WORSE THAN MY CRASH-LANDING. I HOPE THIS SERRATOR CAN **TRANSLATE** YOU.>

BE SILENT. WHAT WERE YOU JUST **PLANTING** THERE?
UH... NOTHING?

BUSHIGAL! I KNOW MORGANA'S MAGIKS WHEN I SEE THEM!
FWA-WHAM
SWEET SEKLOS!

BACK OFF!
LOOK, OBVIOUSLY I'M NEW HERE! I DON'T KNOW WHO YOU ARE OR WHAT YOUR PROBLEM IS--

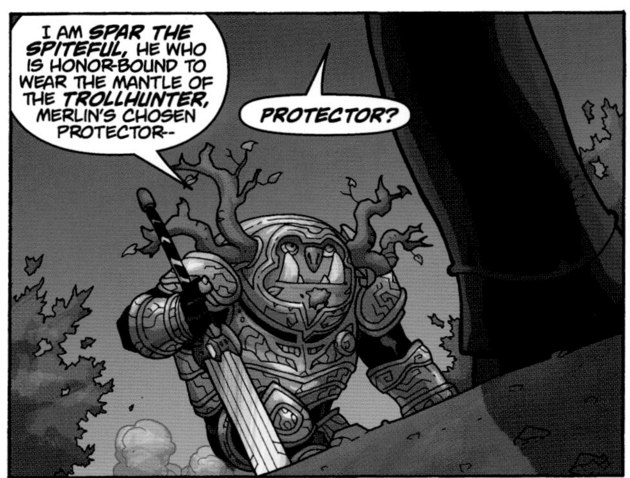
I AM SPAR THE SPITEFUL, HE WHO IS HONOR-BOUND TO WEAR THE MANTLE OF THE TROLLHUNTER, MERLIN'S CHOSEN PROTECTOR--
PROTECTOR?

THEN WE ARE ONE AND THE SAME!
I WAS SENT BY MY HOMEWORLD, AKIRIDION-5, TO SCOUT ANY PLANETS PRIMITIVE ENOUGH TO UNKNOWINGLY SAFEGUARD OUR--
PRIMITIVE?! WHO'RE YOU CALLING--

RRRAAAAA!
BY THE VENTIS! WHAT IS THAT? SOME SORT OF INDIGENOUS DEATH-BRINGER?
WORSE...

FLESHBAGS.

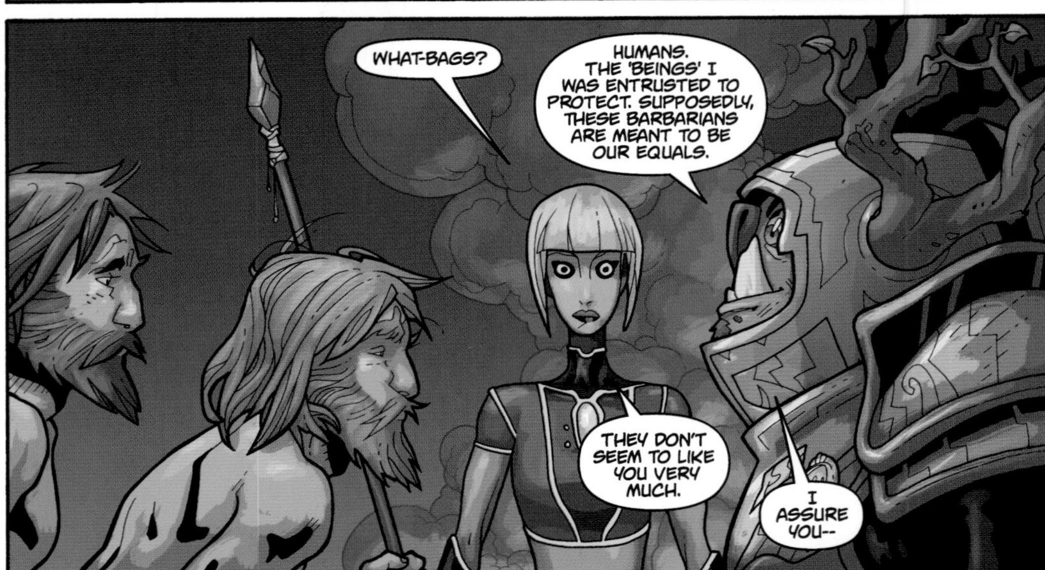
WHAT-BAGS?
HUMANS. THE 'BEINGS' I WAS ENTRUSTED TO PROTECT. SUPPOSEDLY, THESE BARBARIANS ARE MEANT TO BE OUR EQUALS.
THEY DON'T SEEM TO LIKE YOU VERY MUCH.
I ASSURE YOU--

PEK
--THE FEELING IS *MUTUAL.*
POK

BAH!
THAT'S IT-- RUN! JUST BECAUSE I SAVE YOUR SORRY HIDES DOESN'T MEAN I HAVE TO LIKE YOU!

BZZAKT
KLEB!

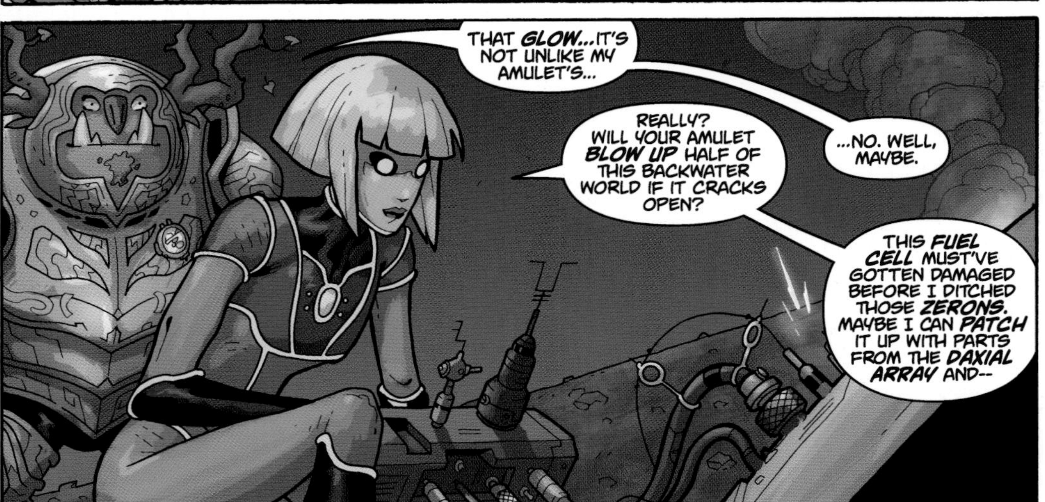
THAT GLOW...IT'S NOT UNLIKE MY AMULET'S...
REALLY? WILL YOUR AMULET BLOW UP HALF OF THIS BACKWATER WORLD IF IT CRACKS OPEN?
...NO. WELL, MAYBE.
THIS FUEL CELL MUST'VE GOTTEN DAMAGED BEFORE I DITCHED THOSE ZERONS. MAYBE I CAN PATCH IT UP WITH PARTS FROM THE DAXIAL ARRAY AND--

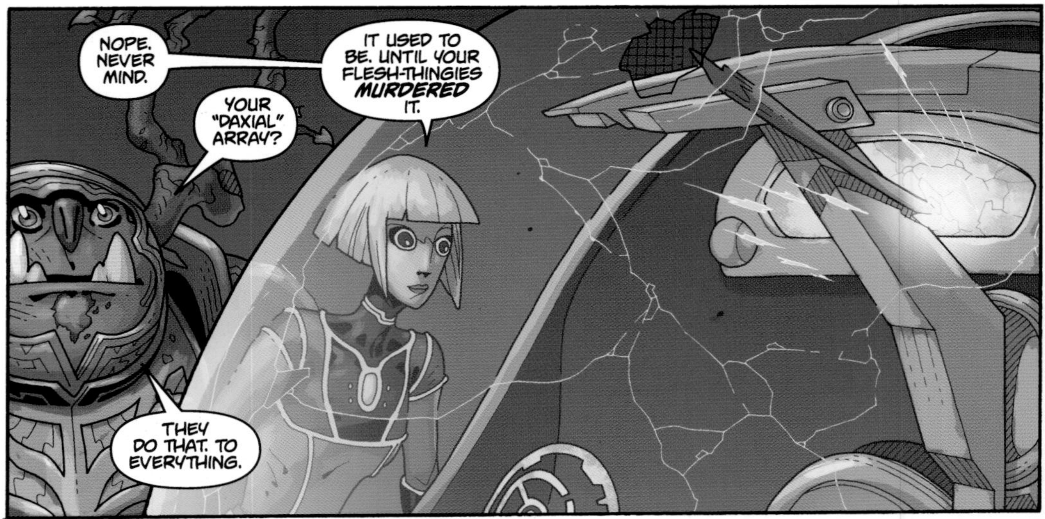
NOPE. NEVER MIND.
YOUR "DAXIAL" ARRAY?
IT USED TO BE. UNTIL YOUR FLESH-THINGIES MURDERED IT.
THEY DO THAT. TO EVERYTHING.

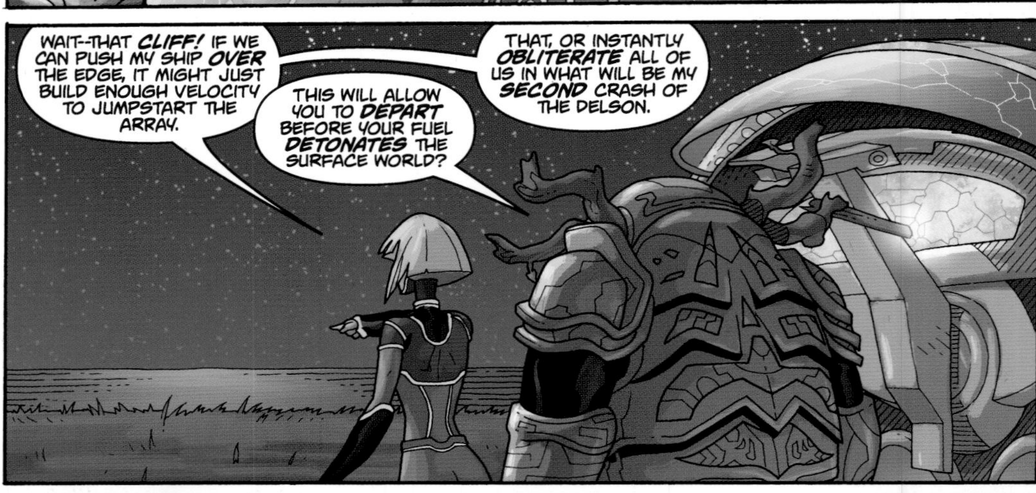
WAIT--THAT CLIFF! IF WE CAN PUSH MY SHIP OVER THE EDGE, IT MIGHT JUST BUILD ENOUGH VELOCITY TO JUMPSTART THE ARRAY.
THIS WILL ALLOW YOU TO DEPART BEFORE YOUR FUEL DETONATES THE SURFACE WORLD?
THAT, OR INSTANTLY OBLITERATE ALL OF US IN WHAT WILL BE MY SECOND CRASH OF THE DELSON.

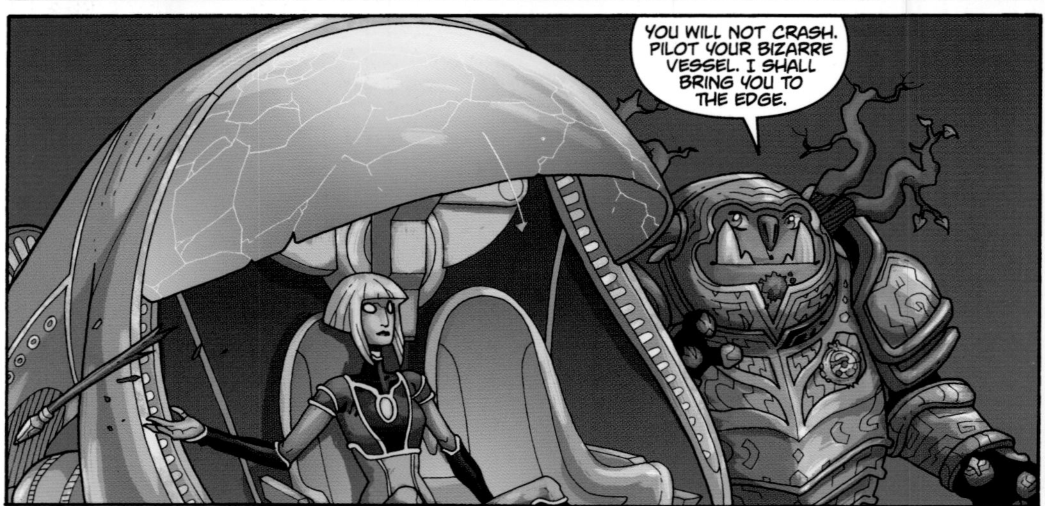
YOU WILL NOT CRASH. PILOT YOUR BIZARRE VESSEL. I SHALL BRING YOU TO THE EDGE.

NNN! THIS WEIGHS MORE THAN A MOUNTAIN TROLL! MOVE, BLAST YOU! MO--

--HUH?

THAT'S IT! PUT YOUR BACKS INTO IT, ALL OF YOU! PUSH!

YOU...YOU DID WELL, FLESHBA-- HUMANS. LET US PRAY TO GORGUS THAT IT WAS ENOUGH TO--

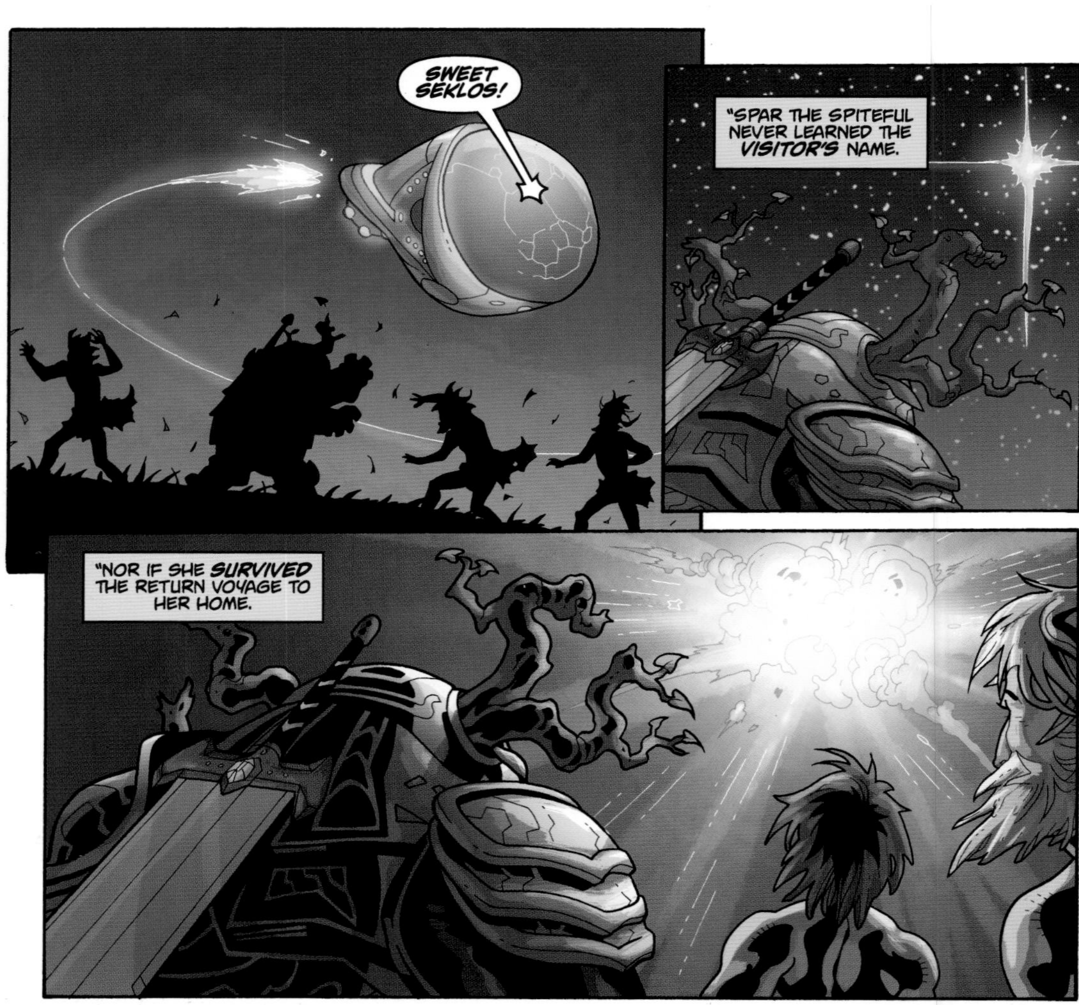
SWEET SEKLOS!
"SPAR THE SPITEFUL NEVER LEARNED THE VISITOR'S NAME.
"NOR IF SHE SURVIVED THE RETURN VOYAGE TO HER HOME.

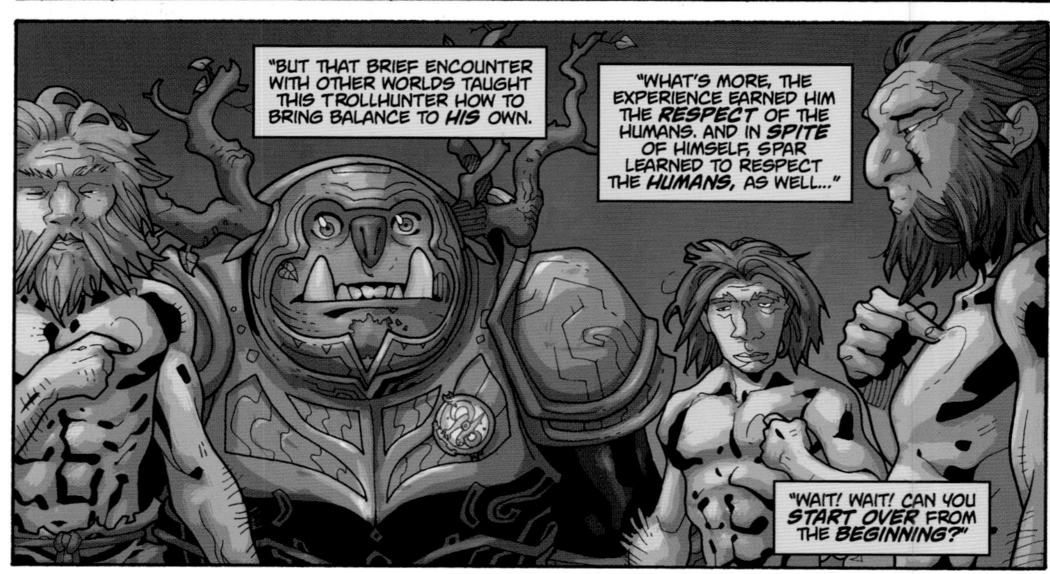
"BUT THAT BRIEF ENCOUNTER WITH OTHER WORLDS TAUGHT THIS TROLLHUNTER HOW TO BRING BALANCE TO HIS OWN.
"WHAT'S MORE, THE EXPERIENCE EARNED HIM THE RESPECT OF THE HUMANS. AND IN SPITE OF HIMSELF, SPAR LEARNED TO RESPECT THE HUMANS, AS WELL..."
"WAIT! WAIT! CAN YOU START OVER FROM THE BEGINNING?"

I DIDN'T REALIZE THE LITTLE TROLL ROOM'S SO FAR AWAY!
PATIENCE, TROLLHUNTER. LET'S JUST SAY SOME THINGS ARE NOT MEANT TO BE KNOWN...YET.
AND I WOULD ALSO LOVE FOR YOU TO BACK UP AND EXPLAIN THAT WHOLE "VISITOR FROM ANOTHER WORLD" THING AGAIN!
ISN'T THAT RIGHT, BLINKOUS? AARGHAUMONT?

"NOW WHERE IN GIZMODIUS' NAME HAVE THEY DISAPPEARED TO?"

BLINKY'S LIBRARY?
THE HERO'S FORGE?
SOMEHOW, I VERY MUCH DOUBT THAT. WHAT A PITY. THE ANAMNESIS STONE IS NOW ABOUT TO REVEAL THE LEGEND OF ANOTHER TROLLHUNTER.
ONE WHO ALSO HAPPENS TO BE ONE OF BLINKY'S RELATIVES...

"ARAKNAK THE AGILE!"
HA HA!

VERILY, YOU GRUESOMES HAD BEST SCAVENGE ANOTHER CAVERN FOR A TROLL CARCASS.
I FEEL FAR TOO ALIVE TO FEED YOUR FOUL APPETITES THIS DAY!
ARAKNAK! HAVE A CARE!
STOP SHOWING OFF, SON!

MOM! DAD! WILL YOU TWO PLEASE BUTT OUT? THE TROLLHUNTER ISN'T LIKE YOU!
I'M A BRAWLER, NOT A SCHOLAR. AND THIS ISN'T THE TIME FOR OVER-THINKING--

--THIS IS THE TIME FOR OVER-FIGHTING!
HA! TAKE THAT! AND THAT!
AND THAT AND THAT!
THOK
SHUK
WATCH YOUR FOOTING, ARAKNAK!
DON'T LET THEM SURROUND YOU!

AAAGGH!
SON!
NNN!
SCHLORP

MOM, DAD...DON'T LOOK...

TO HELHEETI WITH THAT.
NO GRUESOME'S GOING TO EAT *MY* BOY IN FRONT OF ME!

THAT WON'T HOLD FOR LONG. THE GRUESOMES WILL EVENTUALLY SLITHER BETWEEN THE CRACKS.
YOU KNOW, THIS IS ONE OF THE REASONS I DON'T WANT YOU ALWAYS FOLLOWING ME ON MY TROLLHUNTS--
--BETWEEN ALL THE VICTORIES, YOU'RE BOUND TO WITNESS THE OCCASIONAL FAILURE.
SO, WHAT, WE SHOULD JUST STAY IN OUR CAVE WHILE OUR ONLY CHILD BLITHELY GALLIVANTS FROM ONE LIFE-OR-DEATH BATTLE TO THE NEXT?
I GUESS WHEN YOU PUT IT THAT WAY...
WHAT A FOOLHARDY NOTION, SON. ALMOST AS FOOLHARDY AS NOT IDENTIFYING THE GRUESOMES' STRIKE PATTERN, THEREBY LETTING THEM CORNER YOU.
SEE?! THIS IS EXACTLY WHAT I'M TALKING ABOUT!
I...I'M NEVER GOING TO MEASURE UP TO YOU. EITHER OF YOU.
THAT'S WHY I CHOSE THE PATH OF THE WARRIOR, NOT THE ACADEMIC...

"MEASURE UP"? SON, YOU'VE ALREADY SURPASSED US BOTH. WE'RE PROUD OF YOU, IN VICTORY AND IN FAILURE.
OUR BOY--NAY, OUR TROLLHUNTER--IS CAPABLE ENOUGH TO WALK BOTH PATHS. AND MANY, MANY MORE, IF HE SO DESIRES.
AWWW, YOU GUYS...

RIGHT NOW, THE ONLY PATH I'M INTERESTED IN IS THE ONE THAT LEADS US SAFELY BACK HOME. BUT THAT MEANS GOING THROUGH THOSE GRUESOMES AGAIN...

ONLY THIS ISN'T THE TIME FOR OVER-FIGHTING...

THEY'RE HERE! MOM, DAD--HIDE!
C'MON, YOU GRUMBLY GRUESOMES. COME FINISH THE REST OF YOUR FEAST. BUT FIRST--

PAFF
PAFF
--ALLOW ME TO PASS THE SALT!
HEY, MOM AND DAD! CHECK THIS OUT! A LITTLE TRICK I PICKED UP FROM MAGMAR THE MOLTEN!
GO, ARAKNAK!
THAT'S MY BOY!
"ARAKNAK THE AGILE WOULD GO ON TO LOSE A FEW MORE APPENDAGES DURING HIS TENURE, YET THE INJURIES DID LITTLE TO DAMPEN HIS CAREFREE ZEAL--
"--OR TO ERASE HIS PARENTS' LESSON THAT THE TROLLHUNTER'S GREATEST WEAPON IS OFTEN THE TROLLHUNTER'S OWN MIND."

INDEED! I NEVER TIRE OF HEARING ABOUT MY ANCESTORS' WIT, CUNNING, AND *HIC* PENCHANT FOR THEATRICS!
AT THE RISK OF IMMODESTY, I DARESAY SOME OF THOSE SKILLS HAVE EVEN PASSED DOWN TO *HIC* ME--

VENDEL, I GET THAT YOU'RE IN A RUSH TO LEAVE--
EH, WHAT'S THE POINT NOW? I DOUBT THERE'S A SINGLE DROP LEFT, JUDGING BY THESE THREE.
--AND I GET THAT MY MIND CAN BE A GREAT WEAPON. EXCEPT IN MY SPANISH AND ALGEBRA II CLASSES, APPARENTLY.
BUT WHAT HAPPENS WHEN THAT WEAPON GETS TURNED UPON ITSELF?

WH-WHAT IF I LOSE CONTROL OF MY EMOTIONS AND SOME OTHER JIM GETS IN THE DRIVER'S SEAT?
BEEK-A-POO.
IT'S "PEEK-A-BOO." BUT POINTS FOR TRYING!

WILL HE BE A GREATER CHAMPION? OR A GREATER DANGER TO EVERYONE AROUND ME?
HMM. SEEING YOU THERE REMINDS ME OF ANOTHER CHAMPION.
ONE FAMOUS FOR DEEP INTROSPECTION AND QUESTIONING THE TROLLHUNTER'S PLACE IN THE UNIVERSE, EVEN AFTER SHE WON THE BATTLE OF KILLAHEAD BRIDGE...

DEYA? WHAT VEXES YOU OF LATE?

RUNDLE, I REALIZE IT'S ONLY BEEN A CENTURY SINCE THE AMULET SELECTED ME--
BARELY THE BLINK OF A KELPESTRUM'S EYE.
--YET I LONG TO KNOW MY LARGER PURPOSE. MY...DESTINY. IF ONLY THIS AMULET WEREN'T SO SPARING IN REVEALING ITS MAKER'S SECRETS...
I TIRE OF THESE UNBEARABLE STRETCHES OF SILENCE, PUNCTUATED ONLY BY RIDDLES.

PERHAPS I'D DO WELL TO TAKE MY QUESTIONS STRAIGHT TO THE SOURCE.
DEYA! YOU SEEK MERLIN? THE WIZARD'S BEEN GONE FOR AGES!
"IF SHE HEARD MY FATHER THAT DAY, HER EYES DID NOT SHOW IT. THEN AGAIN...

"THE ONLY COUNSEL DEYA THE DELIVERER EVER HEEDED WERE THE URGINGS OF HER OWN INSTINCTS.
"DURING HER MANY TRAVELS, DEYA LEARNED TO QUIET THE INQUIRING VOICES IN HER HEAD--

"--WHILE QUIETING OTHER DISTRACTING VOICES AS WELL.
"DEYA STOPPED MANY TIMES TO AID OTHER TROLLS IN NEED--

"--AND TO SLAY ANY POOR WRETCHES MISGUIDED ENOUGH TO IMPEDE HER QUEST.
"UNTIL ONE DAY, WHEN--WITHOUT ANY INDICATION FROM THE INSCRUTABLE AMULET--THE TROLLHUNTER KNEW IN HER HEART...

"...THE JOURNEY HAD REACHED ITS END."

MERLIN?
OH, GOOD--

-I'VE BEEN EXPECTING YOU.
YOU...YOU HAVE?
OH, DO ME A FAVOR AND LEAVE THIS BAG ON THE FLOOR RIGHT THERE, WOULD YOU?

WHAT.

PERFECT. THANKS. AND BEFORE YOU EVEN ASK--NO, OF COURSE I CAN'T TELL YOU WHAT ULTIMATE PART YOU PLAY IN MY GRAND DESIGNS.
THUD.

REALLY? THEN, TELL ME, WIZARD--
--DID YOU EXPECT THIS?
THWOK

NO, AS A MATTER OF FACT. I DID NOT. HOW CURIOUS...
YOU LET ME TREK ALL THAT TIME, ALL THIS WAY TO YOUR...YOUR RETREAT!
YOU LEFT MY PRAYERS FOR KNOWLEDGE UNANSWERED YEAR AFTER YEAR, ONLY TO DENY ME NOW!

AND?

DO NOT MISUNDERSTAND, TROLLHUNTER. I'M MORE IMPRESSED THAN ANGERED.
TO SEE MY LATEST CREATION BECOME SO FORMIDABLE SO SOON IS AS PLEASANTLY UNEXPECTED AS YOUR FIST.
YOU STILL MANAGE TO SURPRISE ME, CHAMPION.

I TAKE LITTLE COMFORT IN THAT. AND I'VE HAD ENOUGH OF SURPRISES.

FAR BE IT FROM YOU TO IMPART ANY ACTUAL WISDOM, BUT TROLL LORE TELLS OF A GEMSTONE, INDIGO IN COLOR, WHICH GRANTS THE POWER TO GLIMPSE INTO AN ENEMY'S MIND.
NO! THE OMNISCIENSTONE! TO WIELD IT WITHOUT PREPARATION IS TO COURT MADNESS!
AND?

"IN AN INSTANT, DEYA'S MIND EXPERIENCED THE ANSWERS TO HER EVERY QUESTION. AND TO ONES SHE NEVER DARED ASK...
"SHE SAW TIME AS MERLIN DID--ALL AT ONCE. EVENTS THAT HAD ALREADY TRANSPIRED LONG AGO...
"EVENTS THAT WOULD NOT--OR SHOULD NOT--OCCUR...

"AND EVENTS TOO HORRIFIC TO COMPREHEND THAT, NONETHELESS, MIGHT YET STILL COME TO PASS..."

NO!

WIZARD, I... I'M SOR--
DON'T.

IT IS *I* WHO SHOULD BEG FORGIVENESS. I NEVER MEANT TO *WITHHOLD* DETAILS CAPRICIOUSLY.
I MERELY SOUGHT TO *SPARE* MY CHAMPIONS THE TERRIBLE, OVERWHELMING *DREAD* THAT COMES WITH *UNDERSTANDING*. TO PRESERVE THEIR--*YOUR*--SANITY.

PERHAPS YOU MIGHT EXPLAIN THAT TO YOUR NEXT TROLLHUNTER. IF... IF IT PLEASES YOU.
BUT I SPEAK OUT OF TURN.
I SEE NOW THAT MY PLACE IS TO FOLLOW ORDERS, NOT COMPREHEND THEM.
THIS IS A FINE DESTINY, AND I SHALL ENDEAVOR TO EARN IT, ONE HUNT AT A TIME.
ON THE CONTRARY...

LIKE YOU, I HAVE SEEN THE FUTURE. THUS, I KNOW YOUR TRUE FATE IS TO LEAD, NOT FOLLOW.
TAKE HEART, DEYA, AND TRUST THAT--ALTHOUGH YOU MAY NEVER PERCEIVE ALL THE PROBABILITIES CHURNING ABOUT YOU...

"IN TIMES OF GREATEST NEED, IT IS YOU WHO SHALL DELIVER TROLLKIND INTO TOMORROW..."

WOW. WHO KNEW DEYA HAD SUCH A PROBLEM WITH AUTHORITY FIGURES?
I GUESS NOW I DON'T FEEL SO BAD ABOUT WANTING TO HURT STRICKLER...
BUT...BUT DEYA NEVER REALLY DOUBTED HERSELF, DID SHE? EVEN WHEN SHE CHALLENGED MERLIN, SHE WAS SO DECISIVE, SO SURE OF HERSELF.

SO UNLIKE ME. WHAT...WHAT DO YOU THINK THAT MEANS, VENDEL?
WHAT DO YOU THINK IT MEANS?

THAT I SHOULD BE A WHOLE LOT MORE SURE OF MYSELF?
PERHAPS. ALTHOUGH I'D CAUTION AGAINST BECOMING TOO SURE. SUCH OVERCONFIDENCE LEADS ONLY TO FOLLY. IT CERTAINLY DID FOR--

"--UNKAR THE UNFORTUNATE!"
AT LAST!
TODAY, THE AMULET'S FINALLY CHOSEN THE ONE SOUL INTREPID ENOUGH TO TRULY DESERVE IT--ME!

FORGET BORAZ THE BOLD OR TELLAD-URR THE TERRIBLE. "OH, POOR ME! I DON'T WANT TO BE MERLIN'S CHAMPION!" PFFT!
I'VE ALWAYS WANTED TO WEAR THIS ARMOR! TO PROVE TO EVERYONE ELSE I'M BRAVE AND WORTHY! I DON'T EVEN NEED BLINKY'S POOR EXCUSE FOR TRAINING!

LEARN MY NAME AND LEARN IT WELL, YOU CURS! FOR TO UTTER IT IS TO KNOW GREATNESS!
I AM UNKAR THE UNBEATABLE! UNKAR THE ULTIMATE!

UNKAR THE--

--UH-OH.

UGH! POOR UNKAR!
NOT THAT I WANT TO GET INTO THE GORY DETAILS, BUT AAARRRGGHH!!! SAID UNKAR WAS TORN LIMB FROM LIMB!

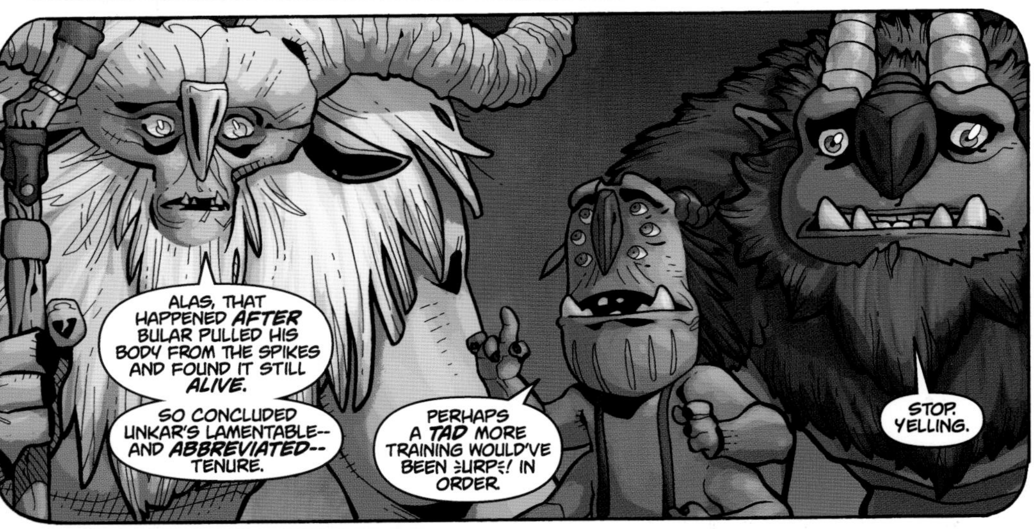
ALAS, THAT HAPPENED AFTER BULAR PULLED HIS BODY FROM THE SPIKES AND FOUND IT STILL ALIVE.
SO CONCLUDED UNKAR'S LAMENTABLE--AND ABBREVIATED--TENURE.
PERHAPS A TAD MORE TRAINING WOULD'VE BEEN URP! IN ORDER.
STOP. YELLING.

UMBRAGE! UMBRAGE, I SAY!
THAT'S HOW THEY REMEMBER ME? WHAT ABOUT THE TWENTY-TWO HOURS WHERE I DIDN'T DIE?!
IF I EVER GET OUTTA THIS VOID, I'M GONNA GIVE THAT HUMAN KID A PIECE OF MY MIND!

LOOK, VENDEL, IT'S NOT THAT I DON'T APPRECIATE YOU SHARING ALL OF THIS HISTORY WITH ME.
BUT HEARING ABOUT ALL OF THESE OTHER TROLLHUNTERS HAS ME FEELING MORE CONFUSED THAN BEFORE!

EACH CHAMPION IS SO DIFFERENT THAN THE ONES WHO CAME BEFORE AND AFTER HIM OR HER. AND NONE OF THEM SEEM LIKE ME AT ALL.
WHAT'S THE TAKEAWAY HERE? THAT I'M DOOMED TO BE THE ONE TROLLHUNTER WHO'S SO BUSY FIGHTING HIMSELF, GUNMAR CAN JUST KICK BACK AND RELAX?

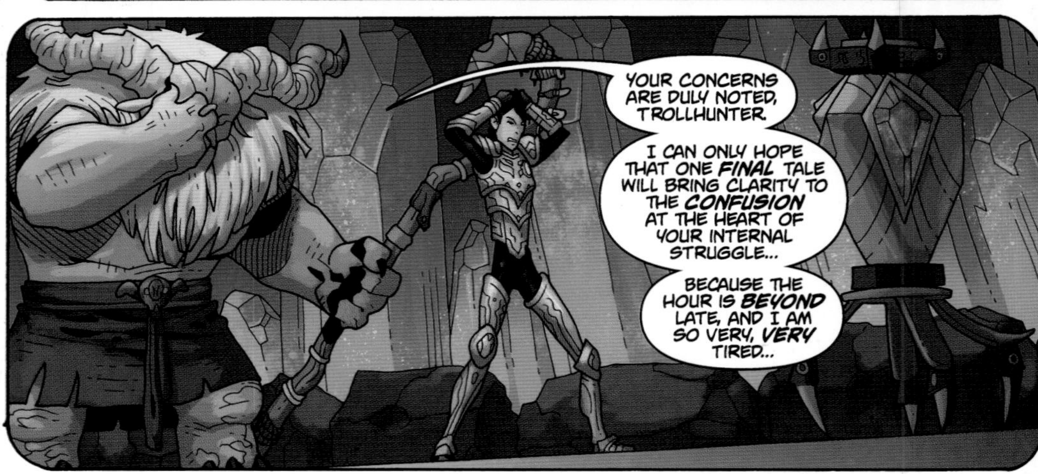
YOUR CONCERNS ARE DULY NOTED, TROLLHUNTER.
I CAN ONLY HOPE THAT ONE FINAL TALE WILL BRING CLARITY TO THE CONFUSION AT THE HEART OF YOUR INTERNAL STRUGGLE...
BECAUSE THE HOUR IS BEYOND LATE, AND I AM SO VERY, VERY TIRED...

"SO HEAR THE TALE FROM KANJIGAR HIMSELF."
HEARTSTONE TROLLMARKET, SUMMER OF FIFTY-THREE. ON THE HUMAN CALENDAR, ANYWAY.
HOTTEST YEAR ON RECORD. AT LEAST, THAT WAS THE WORD ON THE SURFACE. BUT DOWN HERE--
--IT FELT A LOT HOTTER.
KANJIGAR THE COURAGEOUS?
NOBODY CALLED ME THAT ANYMORE. NOT SINCE THE WAR.

WHAT BRINGS A BEAUTIFUL RIVER TROLL LIKE YOU TO THIS PART OF THE MARKET?
BLASTED SCORCH BEETLES!
FOUND THESE IN HUMAN DUMPSTER. PRETTY?
IT'S MY SISTER. MY TWIN SISTER, SHMORKRARG. SHE'S GONE MISSING.
THIS TWIN SISTER OF YOURS HAVE ANY ENEMIES?
SAME ENEMIES AS ANY RIVER TROLL HAS, I SUPPOSE-- THE GARDEN TROLLS.
GREAT GRONKA MORKA!

SHE...SHE'S ALL I HAVE LEFT IN THE WORLD. WE LOST OUR FAMILY IN THE KELPESTRUM QUAKE LAST CENTURY.
IF YOU COULD DO ANYTHING TO HELP FIND MY SISTER, I'D BE SO VERY... APPRECIATIVE.
THEN CONSIDER ME ON THE HUNT, MISSUS...?

IT'S MISS. TRADNARA. BUT YOU CAN CALL ME "NARA."
NARA. TROLLSPEAK FOR "TROUBLE" WITH A CAPITAL T.
KANJIGAR, MY OLD FRIEND, I MEAN NO OFFENSE--
--BUT HAVE YOU TAKEN LEAVE OF YOUR SENSES?! THE RIVER AND GARDEN TROLLS HAVE FEUDED FOR MILLENNIA, LIKE... LIKE...

HATFIELDS AND MCCOYS?
I HAVE NO IDEA WHAT THOSE ARE. BUT, YES, LIKE THEM!
ANYONE CAUGHT IN THE CROSSFIRE HASN'T LIVED LONG ENOUGH TO REGRET IT! I BESEECH YOU, DO NOT INTERFERE IN THEIR AFFAIRS.

IT'S THE JOB. YOU TWO MIGHT BE HAPPY DUSTING BOOKS AND SIFTING THROUGH GARBAGE, BUT NOT I. NOT AFTER WHAT...
NOT AFTER. IF YOU WON'T STAY QUIET ABOUT YOUR FEARS, THEN STAY BEHIND. I CAN DO THIS ALONE!
IT WAS A LIE. THEN AGAIN, THE TRUTH AND I WEREN'T EXACTLY ON SPEAKING TERMS.
BUT IF I WAS ABOUT TO KICK A PIXIE NEST, THEN I STILL NEEDED--

--BACKUP.
--WOULD NEVER SIDE WITH ANY OVER YOU. AND YET, I MUST ADMIT YOU'VE BEEN DIFFERENT SINCE THE GREAT ROCKY MOUNTAIN TROLL WAR. LONELIER.
THAT IS TO SAY, I REALIZE SOME TIME HAS PASSED SINCE YOU AND MOTHER--
DON'T BRING HER MEMORY INTO THIS, DRAAL. WE'RE ON A BEAT. BESIDES...

...I'VE NEVER QUESTIONED YOUR ROMANTIC TASTES.
FATHER... THAT'S NOT FAIR. NOMURA AND I ARE--
BUSHIGAL!

THIS RAVINE IS A GARDEN, ALBEIT A MARSHY ONE! AS SUCH, IT'S THE RIGHTFUL TERRITORY OF WE GARDEN TROLLS!
AND THE RIVER TROLLS CLAIM THIS CHANNEL AS A RIVER! MODEST THOUGH IT MAY BE, WETLANDS SUCH AS THESE HAVE ALWAYS BEEN OUR PROVINCE.
IS THAT WHY YOU SILT-SUCKERS SET OUR CRYSTAL ORCHARDS ABLAZE?
ONLY AFTER YOU BRANCH-BRAINED TWITS SALTED OUR STREAMS!

ENOUGH!
I KNOW NOT WHAT BEGAT THIS SENSELESS GRUDGE IN THE OLD WORLD, BUT WE NOW OCCUPY A NEW ONE.
WE MUST ALL ADAPT TO THESE NEW SURROUNDINGS. LEARN TO EXIST ALONGSIDE THE HUMANS--AND EACH OTHER!
AND WHY SHOULD OUR TROLLHUNTER CARE NOW OF ALL TIMES?
LAST WE HEARD, YOU WERE STILL NURSING OLD WOUNDS AT THE BOTTOM OF A GLUG JUG.
STAY YOUR TONGUE, IMBECILE, LEST I CARVE IT FROM YOUR HOLLOW SKULL.
I COME IN SEARCH OF ONE OF YOUR KIND NAMED SHMORKRARG. HER TWIN, TRADNARA, HAS HIRED ME TO--
"SHMORKRARG?!" WE HAVE NO SHMORKRARG IN OUR NUMBER
BUT IF IT'S NARA YOU SEEK, YOU'LL FIND HER--
--UP THERE!
NARA?
MY COURAGEOUS KANJIGAR. I DO HOPE YOU'LL FORGIVE ME FOR MISLEADING YOU. AND FOR THIS.

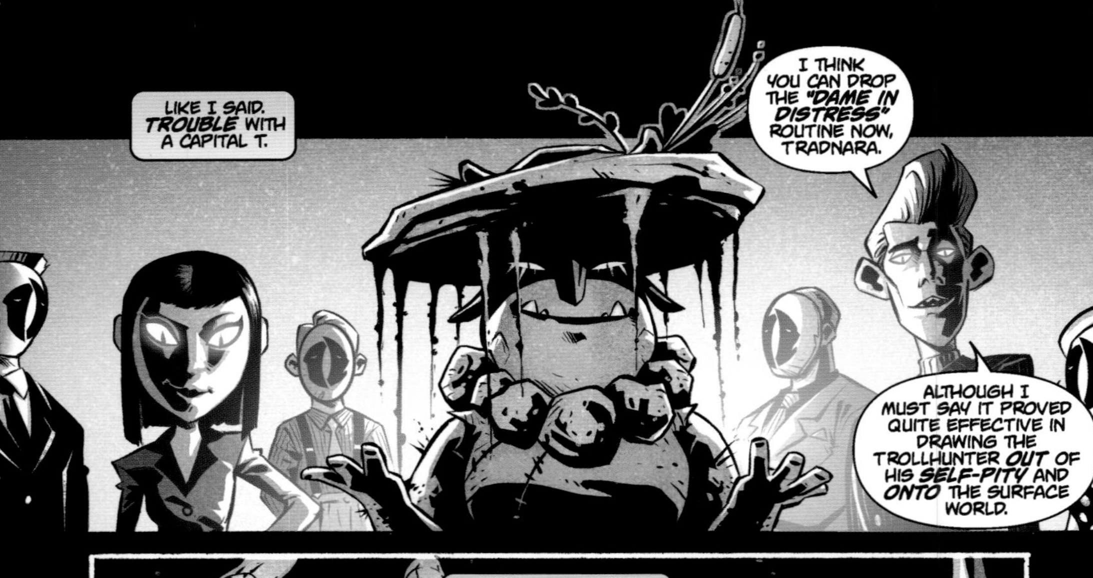
LIKE I SAID. TROUBLE WITH A CAPITAL T.
I THINK YOU CAN DROP THE "DAME IN DISTRESS" ROUTINE NOW, TRADNARA.
ALTHOUGH I MUST SAY IT PROVED QUITE EFFECTIVE IN DRAWING THE TROLLHUNTER OUT OF HIS SELF-PITY AND ONTO THE SURFACE WORLD.

AND SHE'D BEEN PLAYING ME LIKE A GORB AT THE ANNUAL PYROBLIGST FINALS.
NOMURA?

GROW UP, DRAAL. WE WERE NEVER MEANT TO LAST. THIS IS BIGGER THAN US. IT'S BUSINESS--
--NOTHING PERSONAL!
SEEING NARA SIDE WITH THOSE CHANGELINGS HURT MORE THAN ANY GRENADE COULD'VE--

KA
THOOM

--EVEN WHEN ITS SHRAPNEL'S BEEN LACED WITH CREEPER'S SUN.
SPA
TANG
BOOM
THIS WAS ALL JUST A TRAP. PLAIN AND SIMPLE. AND SHE LED ME BY MY NOSE RING RIGHT INTO IT.
RRRAAAAAHHH!
THE JANUS ORDER FINALLY RAN OUT OF DWÄRKSTONE, BUT I STILL TASTED CINDERS ON MY TONGUE. AND SOMETHING EVEN MORE BITTER
THE AMBUSH. THE RIVER AND GARDEN TROLLS' FEUD. CHOOSING MY EGO OVER MY FRIENDS. IT ALL SEEMED SO SENSELESS NOW.

I...I'LL BE JOINING YOU NOW, SISTER...
NARA!
BUT MERLIN NEVER SAID TROLLHUNTING WAS FAIR.
CONSIDER THIS ESCAPE THE LAST OF MY GIFTS TO YOU, IMPURE.
FATHER, THE OTHER TROLLS-- THEY'VE GONE BACK TO QUARRELING. WHAT WOULD YOU HAVE US DO?
LET THEM FIGHT. THE MORE I TRY TO FIX THINGS, THE MORE HARM I SEEM TO DO.
I HEAR THE BOY'S PROTEST STICK IN HIS THROAT. IT SAVES ME THE EFFORT OF TELLING HIM THE TRUTH:
FORGET IT, DRAAL. IT'S ARCADIA.

THAT'S THE ENDING?
GOTTA SAY, VENDEL, THAT ONE WAS KIND OF A DOWNER. IS TROLL THERAPY ALWAYS SO...GRIM?

YES.
TROLLS NOT BIG ON SHARING.
I CAN SEE WHY...

VENDEL, IF I MAY FURTHER ELUCIDATE THE MEANING OF KANJIGAR'S PARABLE?
GO NUTS.

YOU SEE, MASTER JIM, YOUR PREDECESSOR RECOGNIZED THAT ANY ATTEMPT TO RECONCILE DIFFERENT SIDES IN A CONFLICT SOMETIMES JUST ADDS "FLU TO THE FIRE."
DON'T YOU MEAN "FUEL TO THE FIRE," BLINK?
AH, THAT HUMAN PHRASE MAKES MUCH MORE SENSE NOW. THANK YOU, TOBIAS.
DE NADA.

THE POINT BEING--KANJIGAR LEARNED IT IS OFTEN WISER TO SIMPLY ACCEPT THE CONTRADICTIONS FOUND IN LIFE.

AND FOUND INSIDE EACH OF US...
JUST SO, TROLLHUNTER.

LOOK AT HOW MADDRUX THE MANY WAS BOTH CONFIDENT, YET HUMBLED.

SPAR THE SPITEFUL WAS DEFIANT, YET COMPASSIONATE.

ARAKNAK THE AGILE WAS FORMIDABLE, YET THOUGHTFUL.

DEYA THE DELIVERER WAS *HEADSTRONG,* YET *PATIENT.*

UNKAR WAS...WELL, *UNKAR.*

AND KANJIGAR THE COURAGEOUS WAS *PRINCIPLED,* YET *PRAGMATIC.*

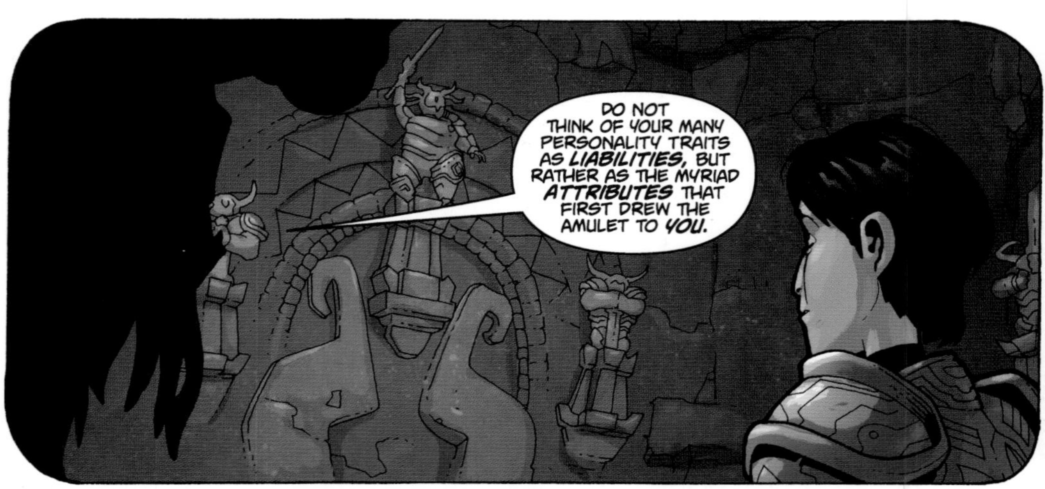
DO NOT THINK OF YOUR MANY PERSONALITY TRAITS AS LIABILITIES, BUT RATHER AS THE MYRIAD ATTRIBUTES THAT FIRST DREW THE AMULET TO YOU.

RATHER THAN FIGHT THE VOICES IN YOUR HEAD AND HEART, EMBRACE THEM, TROLLHUNTER.

OTHERWISE, YOU WILL HAVE WASTED MY ONE NIGHT OFF FOR NOTHING...

FEELING ANY BETTER?
I DUNNO. MAYBE? I...I GUESS I'M JUST HOPING MY GOOD SIDES OUTWEIGH MY BAD SIDES, IF THAT MAKES ANY SENSE.
PRETTY SURE THAT'S CALLED "BEING A TEENAGER," JIMBO. SPEAKING OF, I KINDA SORTA PROMISED DARCI I'D JOIN HER FOR A DANGER HOUSE MARATHON TONIGHT, SO...
LATER, TOBES. HAVE FUN.

SIGH I WONDER WHAT THEY'LL WIND UP CALLING ME...
"JIM THE JITTERY?" "JIM THE JUST?"
TICK
TING

WAKA CHAKA!
WAKA CHAKA!
I'M GUESSING IT'S GONNA BE "JIM THE JINXED."
FOR THE GLORY OF MERLIN--
WAKA CHAKA!

--DAYLIGHT IS MINE TO COMMAND!
"CONFIDENT, YET HUMBLED.

"DEFIANT, YET COMPASSIONATE.

"FORMIDABLE, YET THOUGHTFUL.

"HEADSTRONG, YET PATIENT.
"PRINCIPLED, YET PRAGMATIC."

TAK

ARE YOU CRAZY?!

MY PARENTS WILL KILL YOU IF THEY SEE YOU HERE, JIM!
I KNOW! PART OF ME THOUGHT IT WAS A BAD IDEA TO COME HERE THIS LATE, CLAIRE.
BUT THEN THE OTHER PARTS OF ME THOUGHT THAT FIRST PART WAS AN IDIOT.
HUH?
NEVER MIND. SO, THERE'S THIS SERIOUS GOBLIN INFESTATION ON MAIN STREET AND...WELL, I THOUGHT IT MIGHT BE MORE FUN IF MAYBE I WIPED 'EM ALL OUT ALONGSIDE MY, Y'KNOW--

"--GIRLFRIEND."
CAN'T THINK OF ANYWHERE ELSE I'D RATHER BE, LAKE.
THE END.